A Gift For:

_____

From:

Copyright © 2021 Hallmark Licensing, LLC

Published by Hallmark Gift Books,
a division of Hallmark Cards, Inc.,
Kansas City, MO 64141
Visit us online at Hallmark.com.

Editorial Director: Kara Goodier
Editor: Jake Gahr
Art Director: Amy Abernathy
Designer: Becky Hottel

ISBN: 978-1-63059-525-8
KCX1075

Made in China
0422

Snow Many Treats to Share!

A Snowy Day of Tasty Traditions

Hallmark

A STORY FROM THE HALLMARK HOLIDAY SERIES
Written by Kat Stano Saura   Illustrated by Tom Patrick

When the flakes in Le Flurry came down in a hurry,
the city was coated in snow.
A blizzard was brewing with snowpeople stewing
'cause snowone could get out and go!

In a ten-story high-rise on Iceway and Main
lived a snowgirl who felt quite upset.
"Being stuck for a week feels especially bleak!"
said a totally fretting Snowsette.

"Maybe I'll make the apartment a lake
and skate all around in my socks.
Or maybe I'll chill by this bright windowsill
and arrange my collection of rocks!"

She brainstormed ideas 'til her head became mushy—
then wandered to their kitchenette.
"That's IT!" she exclaimed. "I'll make treats for the neighbors!
Let's DO this thing!" shouted Snowsette.

Opening cupboards and digging through drawers,
she felt like she found hidden treasure.
Then she gathered her family, 'cause it was tradition.
"We'll help you, Snowsette! It's our pleasure!"

When their family recipe cookies and cakes
and cheeseballs and yule logs were done,
Snowsette said, "It's time for my favorite part!
Let's decorate! THAT'S the most fun!"

They added bright sprinkles and sugary twinkles,
then wrapped the sweet treats with a bow,
And Snowsette headed out to make special deliveries
to neighbors upstairs and below!

They met a kind fellow in summertime yellow
who said, "It's a mobile buffet!"
He sampled a pastry and gingerbread roll.
"Here's a chef's kiss for making my day!"

"Monsieur, it's a gift, if you'd please get my drift,"
said Snowsette, sharing treats à la carte.
Then he said, "Have a cookie that looks like yours truly.
I bake them each year, from the heart."

Then they knocked on the door of a party of four—

some roommates who ate all their ramen!

"DUDE . . . you have food! And our stomachs are growling!

And unfortunately, that's quite common."

They gobbled the grub 'til they felt slightly slushy,
then wanted to thank their good guests.
"A traditional toast!" said the nog-loving hosts—
"To sharing with friends—that's the best!"

The next stop was home of a girl named Snowmone
who owned Café Peppermint Puff!
"Each year, I make cookie-dough-cones, my tradition!
Have an order with extra crème fluff!"

Soon, there was honking outside on the curb.

The Jacques CousSnow Fudge Truck was stuck!

"Oh, CREPES!" said Snowsette as she buttoned her coat.

"They're gonna need help . . . AND good luck!"

Snowsette and her fam reached the scene of the jam

and they handed out treats to the crew.

This lifted their spirits and got those wheels spinning.

Jacques said, "We're unstuck 'cause of YOU!"

On their way home, her Aunt AvaBlanche said,
"Snowsette, I'm so proud of you, niece!
You used our traditions to do good for others,
to spread so much friendship and peace!"

Inside, Snowsette witnessed a magical scene,
a party like never before!
The neighbors were swapping their holiday sweets
and no one was bummed anymore!

As they learned new traditions and shared old ones, too,

pure sweetness was all that they felt.

And Snowsette thanked her lucky snowflakes for the way

it totally made her heart melt.

If this chilly adventure
warmed your heart
or if perhaps you just liked the art,
we would love to hear from you.

Please write a review at Hallmark.com,
where you can find more stories
to share and love.

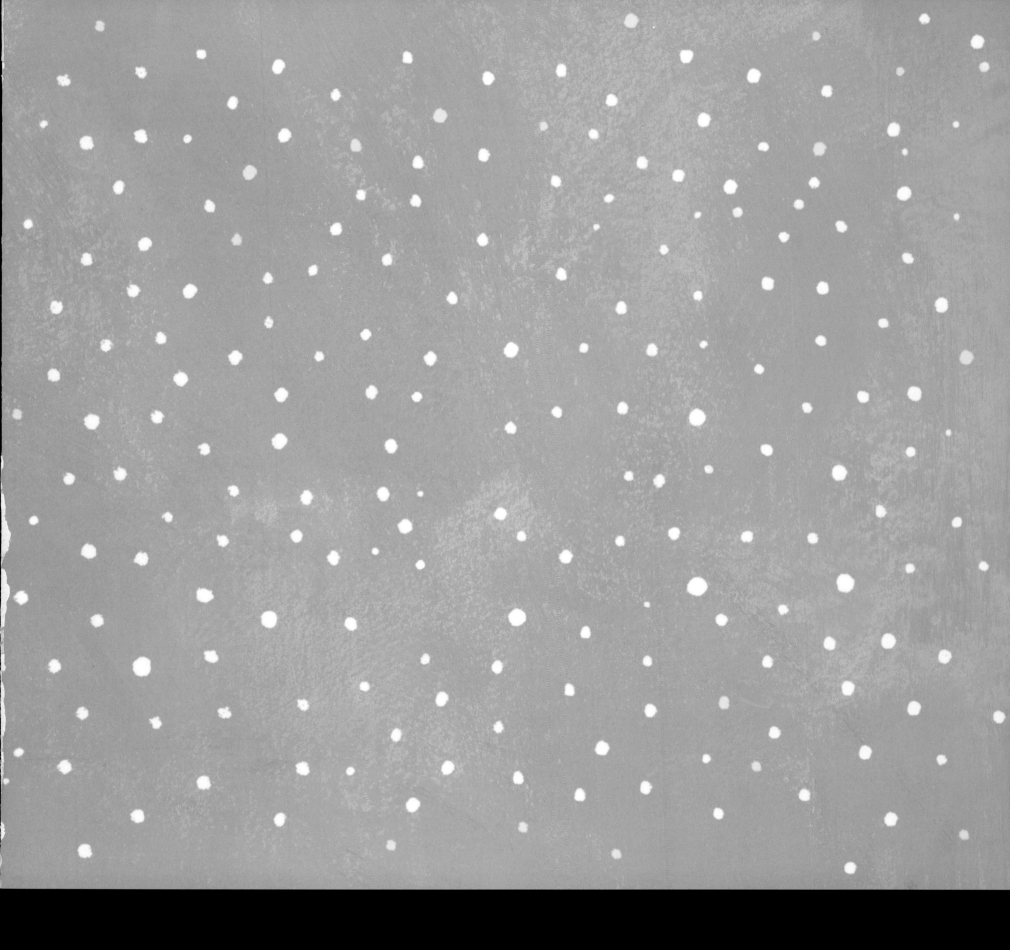